Hoo Hoo Hoo!!!
Merry Christmas!

Written By:
Amanda Kleback

Illustrated By:
Amanda Kleback
& Jessica Lopez

To my Babcia

Hoo Hoo the Bear Company, LLC
Visit http://www.hoohoothebear.com

It was finally Christmas Eve. My belly had looked forward to this day all year.

Mrs. B was busy cooking our Christmas Eve dinner.
The family tradition was to prepare food just like
Mrs.B's grandmother made, and her grandmother
before her. The B women were excellent cooks!

We had fish, potato balls, sauerkraut and fruit soup. FRUIT SOUP!

"Mrs. B, what in the world is fruit soup?," I asked.

"Just you wait, Hoo Hoo, you'll see," said Mrs. B.

It was finally time to eat. The light of the first star shone through the evening sky.

A figure of Baby Jesus lay in a tiny bed of straw on the dinner table as we feasted on what Mrs. B had prepared.

My fuzzy belly was so full!
When dinner was over, I helped Mrs. B clear the table.

"We did not eat all of the fruit soup; what should I do with it?" I asked Mrs. B.
And she said, "Just you wait, Hoo Hoo, you'll see."

After the dishes were cleaned and put away, we gathered around the Christmas tree and talked about all of the visitors we would have the next day.

As I lay by the tree, my fuzzy belly still full, I fell asleep.

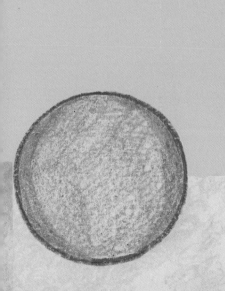

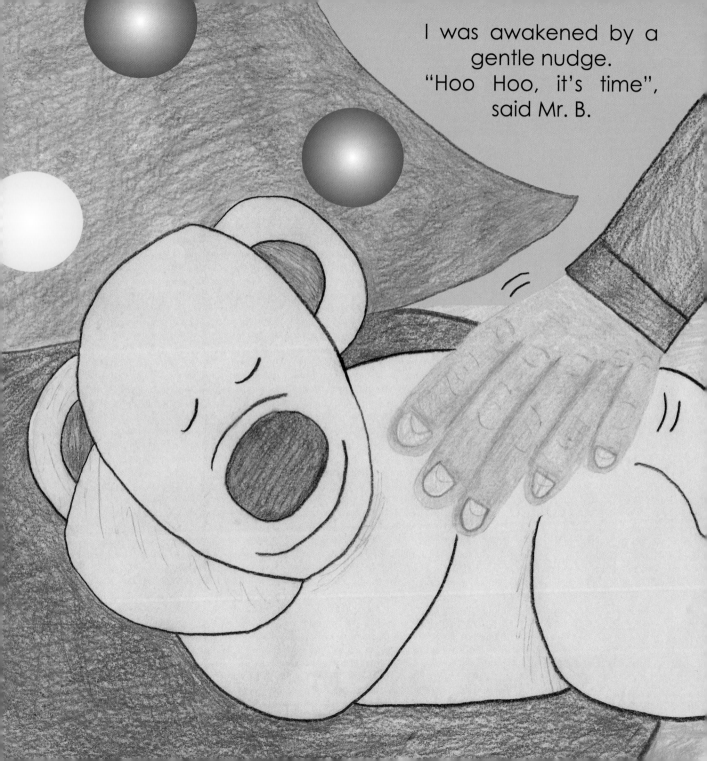

I got up, wiping the sleep from my eyes, and looked at the clock. It was 11:59pm – still Christmas Eve.

Mrs. B said, "Follow me."
Mr. B had the big pot of fruit soup in his
arms and I followed them to the barn.

"We have to hurry, Hoo Hoo", Mr. B said,
"it's almost time."

We pulled the barn door open to see all of the animals waiting. Mr. B poured the fruit soup in each of the animal's food dishes. The momma sheep ate her portion, then looked at us and smiled.

Momma Sheep

Mr. B's watch beep-beep-beeped. It was 12:00am. Christmas Day!

All of a sudden, the barn was flooded with laughter and voices. The animals were talking! It was a miracle!

That year and every Christmas Eve before, Mr. and Mrs. B would take the leftover fruit soup to the animals. This tradition was their way to say "thank you" to the animals for what their ancestors had done for Baby Jesus on that night in the manger so long ago. They protected him from the desert night's chill and helped the angels watch over him.

He is Born

From 12:00am to 12:01am, time stopped for one minute and the animals could talk. They talked for what felt like more than an hour. During that magical minute, we shared stories and talked about the upcoming year.

Mr. B said it was time to go back to the house and go to bed; we had a big day ahead of us.

When I woke up the next morning, I ran past the tree and out the front door to the barn. I flung open the door and went in. "Merry Christmas!", I said, and waited for a reply.

I heard in return, Cock-a-doodle-doo from the rooster,
Hee-haw from the mule,
Moooooo from the cow,
And Baaaah from the momma sheep.

Had I been dreaming last night? I wanted to talk more, I had so much to say...but the animals didn't talk.

I looked at them, disappointed, and said again, "Merry Christmas."

The momma sheep looked at me and smiled.
I knew it! I wasn't dreaming last night! They did talk!

The animals' smiles let me know that we shared the same tradition and love in our hearts. Christmas can indeed be magical–even without saying a word!

Hoo Hoo Hoo!!! Merry Christmas!

Hoo Hoo Hoo! Merry Christmas! is based on the Polish tradition, Wigilia, celebrated by the Author and her family.

Wigilia (Polish pronunciation: [vi'gilja]) is a Polish traditional Christmas Eve supper celebrated by many Polish families around the world. It is held on December 24, Christmas Eve. The term can include the celebration of Midnight Mass, dinner, decorating the Christmas tree, and other traditional family activities.

The word "Wigilia" comes from the Latin verb vigilare, "to watch", and literally means 'eve'. The feasting traditionally begins once the first star has been spotted (usually by children), in the sky at dusk (around 5 p.m.).

Just before the start of dinner, the head of the household will "Break the Bread" with the rest of the table's guests. The "Bread" is a wafer called oplatek (pronounced opwatek) and is the most ancient and beloved of all Polish Christmas traditions. Oplatek is a thin wafer made of flour and water, similar in taste to the hosts that are used for communion during Mass. Wishes for peace and prosperity are exchanged and even the pets and farm animals are given a piece of oplatek on Christmas Eve. One variation of the Wigilia legend and tradition is, instead of fruit soup, the animals eat oplatek on Christmas Eve and can speak in human voices at midnight, and only those who are pure of spirit will be able to hear them.

Foods that are symbolic of what was available in Bethlehem on that sacred night are served. This typically consists of Fish, Potatoes, noodles, other simple vegetables, and of course maybe even fruit soup.

Traditions can vary from community to community. The importance of any variation of Wigilia is that it is a celebration of Family, Friends, and most importantly the Birth of Jesus Christ.